RAINBOW
magic®

The Sporty Fairies

Special thanks to
Narinder Dhami

ORCHARD BOOKS
338 Euston Road, London NW1 3BH
Orchard Books Australia
Level 17/207 Kent Street, Sydney, NSW 2000
A Paperback Original

First published in 2008 by Orchard Books.

A CIP catalogue record for this book is available
from the British Library.

ISBN 978 1 84616 889 5
1 3 5 7 9 10 8 6 4 2

Printed in Great Britain

Orchard Books is a division of Hachette Children's Books,
an Hachette Livre UK company

www.orchardbooks.co.uk

Francesca
the Football
Fairy

by Daisy Meadows

ORCHARD BOOKS

www.rainbowmagic.co.uk

The Fairyland Palace

Fairylan[d]

Car Park

Coaches

Riding Stables

Cooke Football Stadium

Netball Courts

Football Pitches

Tippington Town

LEISURE CENTRE

Swimming Pool

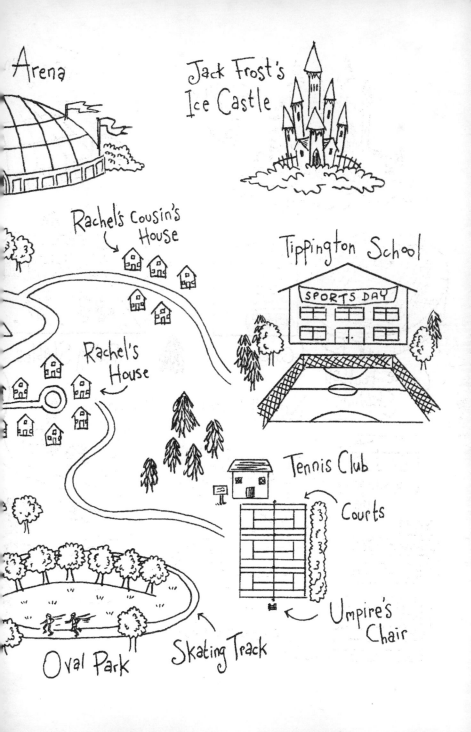

The Fairyland Olympics are about to start,
And my expert goblins are going to take part.
We will win this year, for I've got a cunning plan.
I'm sending my goblins to the arena in Fairyland.

The Magic Sporty Objects that make sports safe and fun,
Will be stolen by my goblins, to keep until we've won.
Sporty Fairies, prepare to lose and to watch us win.
Goblins, follow my commands, and let the games begin!

Contents

Football Fun

"You look great, Dad!" Rachel Walker laughed, glancing at her father as she climbed out of the car. Mr Walker was wearing a blue and white football shirt and scarf, his face was painted with blue and white stripes, and he had a fluffy blue and white wig on his head.

"The wig's fantastic!" Kirsty Tate, Rachel's best friend, added with a grin. She was staying with the Walkers over the spring holiday. "He's going to be the best-dressed Tippington Rovers supporter here."

Rachel nodded. "I'm glad Mum and I are just wearing scarves, though," she added. "That wig looks a bit hot!"

"It is, but I want to show my support for the team," said Mr Walker, as they left the car park and joined the other football fans heading towards the Cooke Stadium. "This is a very important match, girls. If Tippington beat Alton United today, the team will be promoted to the next league!"

Rachel and Kirsty exchanged concerned glances. They were both worried that the football match would be a complete disaster, because the Sporty Fairies had lost their Magic Sporty Objects.

When these special objects were in their proper places, with the Sporty Fairies or in the fairies' lockers, they made sure that sport in both the human and fairy worlds was safe, fun and exciting. Unfortunately, they'd been stolen by cunning Jack Frost and his goblin servants.

Jack Frost was determined to win the Fairyland Olympics, which started in six days' time, and so he'd ordered his goblins to hide the objects away in the human world until the games took place. Then, by keeping the Magic Sporty Objects close to them, the goblins would win every single event. The Fairyland Olympics couldn't be cancelled because that would ruin the Olympic Games in the human world, so Rachel and Kirsty had promised their fairy friends that they would do their best to find the objects before the games took place.

"I'm glad we persuaded Mum and Dad to come to the match early today," Rachel said quietly to Kirsty. "Maybe the goblin who has Francesca the Football Fairy's Magic Football will be here, too."

"Helena the Horseriding Fairy did say that any goblin who has one of the magic objects will be near that sport," Kirsty agreed.

13

The girls had helped Helena to get her Magic Hard Hat back just the day before. "She said that Jack Frost has told the goblins to practise their sporty skills before the Fairyland Olympics, remember?"

"Yes, and King Oberon said that the winning Olympic team will get the Fairyland Olympics Cup, which is filled with luck," Kirsty reminded Rachel. "Think how much more mischief Jack Frost could cause if he had loads of good luck!"

"Girls, come and have your picture taken," called Mrs Walker, holding up her camera.

"Ooh, good idea," Rachel said, as she and Kirsty hurried over to join her parents outside the stadium entrance.

"Then we won't forget how much effort Dad's put into his outfit!"

"I feel like the odd one out," Kirsty joked, as Mrs Walker took their photo. "I'm the only one without any Tippington Rovers colours on."

"There's a kiosk inside the stadium that sells merchandise," Rachel's dad told her. "We'll buy you a scarf there."

"Thank you!" Kirsty exclaimed.

As they went inside the stadium, Rachel immediately started looking around for any sign of goblins, but she didn't see any flashes of goblin green.

Remember, you have to let the magic come to you, Rachel told herself. But she couldn't help hoping that the magic came before the match started, otherwise the game would be ruined.

There weren't many people inside the stadium yet, so there was no queue at the merchandise kiosk. They headed straight over to it, and Mr Walker bought a scarf for Kirsty.

"Here you are, dear," said the shop assistant, popping the scarf into a carrier bag and handing it to Kirsty. "Enjoy the game."

"Thank you," Kirsty said gratefully.

"Let's go and find our seats,"
Mrs Walker suggested.

They all went into the main part
of the stadium, which was still fairly
empty. Kirsty and Rachel had the
chance to take a good look around,
but neither of the girls could see
anything out of the ordinary.

"Maybe we should explore," Kirsty

whispered to Rachel. "There may be
goblin mischief going on somewhere
else."

"Dad, is it OK
if Kirsty and I go
and look around?"
asked Rachel.

"That's fine,"
Mr Walker
replied, settling
himself in his seat.
"We'll sit and watch
the pre-match build-up on the giant
TV screens."

"Just make sure you're back before
the match starts," Rachel's mum added.

The girls nodded.

"I'll put my new scarf on," Kirsty
said, as she and Rachel hurried off.

She opened the bag, and a cloud of glittering sparkles immediately burst from inside. Then, as both girls stared in surprise, the scarf snaked gracefully out of the bag, with a tiny fairy perched daintily on the end of it!

Commentary Confusion

"It's Francesca the Football Fairy!"
Kirsty cried in delight.

"Hello, girls!" Francesca called. She
wore a green and yellow football shirt
with matching shorts and football boots,
and her long hair was braided and tied
back in a ponytail. She hovered in the
air in front of the girls as the scarf

settled around Kirsty's neck. "I have
a feeling those very unsporting goblins
may be here!" she added.

"We've been looking out for them,"
Rachel told her, "but we haven't seen
any yet…"

Suddenly, one of the stadium officials
came running towards them. Francesca
quickly hid behind a fold of Kirsty's scarf,
but the official was too busy speaking
into a walkie-talkie to notice her.

"Yes, all the footballs in the stadium have vanished!" he exclaimed. "If we don't find one – and soon – the game will have to be cancelled!" And, with that, he disappeared into the players' tunnel.

"Hmm. Missing footballs! This has goblin mischief written all over it," Francesca said.

"But why would a goblin have taken all the footballs?" asked Rachel, puzzled.

"Yes, if he's got your Magic Football, why would he need any others?" Kirsty asked.

"I don't know," Francesca replied.

"Well, let's see if we can find the goblin and get the footballs back," Rachel suggested.

Just then, Kirsty's attention was caught by one of the giant TV screens overhead. "Rachel, look," she cried. "There's your dad!"

Rachel glanced up and her face broke into a grin. Mr Walker was on the TV screen, being interviewed by a football commentator.

"So, Mr Walker, what do you think will happen in the game today?" asked the commentator.

"Oh, Tippington Rovers will win!" Rachel's dad replied confidently. "I think the score will be two-nil."

"I like your dad's wig, Rachel!" Francesca chuckled.

The commentator thanked Mr Walker, turned away and headed through the stadium, still talking to the camera.

"OK, girls," Francesca said. "Where shall we look for goblins?"

Just as Kirsty was about to look away from the TV screen, the commentator opened the door of his commentary box and she saw that there was someone inside. A small person wearing a tracksuit, a Tippington Rovers woolly hat and a red Alton United scarf was sitting on the floor, rummaging through a big net filled with footballs.

"Oh, hello," said the commentator, sounding surprised. "Are you here to cover the match with me?"

Curiously, Kirsty stared up at the screen, wondering why all the footballs were hidden away in the commentary box.

The small man looked up irritably at the commentator's words. As he did so, the scarf, which was wrapped around the bottom of his face, slipped, and Kirsty caught a glimpse of green.

"Oh!" she gasped, "There's the goblin!"

"Where?" Rachel and Francesca both said together, looking around.

"Up there," Kirsty told them, pointing at the TV. "He's in the commentary box with all the footballs!"

As Rachel and Francesca glanced up at the screen, the goblin pulled his scarf quickly back into place, but not before Rachel had spotted a green, pointy nose.

"It is the goblin," she agreed. "And the silly thing's wearing both Tippington and Alton colours!"

"Let's head for the commentary box right away," Francesca called, already zooming into the air. "If the goblin's there, then I bet my Magic Football is too!"

Footballs Galore

Francesca and the girls rushed over to the commentary box. Although they couldn't keep their eyes on the TV screens as they ran, the stadium's loudspeaker system meant that they could hear the commentator still trying to talk to the goblin.

"So, Mr...er..." said the commentator,

sounding confused. "Did you say what your name was?"

"No," the goblin snapped rudely.

"Well, who do you think is going to win the match?" the commentator asked.

"Um…" There was a long silence. "…Manchester United?" the goblin said hesitantly.

Francesca, Rachel and Kirsty couldn't help laughing.

"Manchester United aren't even playing today!" the commentator said crossly.

"Well, that was a silly question anyway," the goblin declared with a loud sniff.

"The commentary box is just around the corner," Rachel panted, pointing at a sign on the wall.

Soon the girls were at the bottom of a flight of stairs that led up to the back of the commentary box. Luckily there was nobody else around.

"What do we do now?" asked Kirsty.

They were near another of the giant TV screens and Rachel glanced up at it.

COMMENTARY BOX

The commentator was spluttering, "Right, and, er...now back to the studio!" Meanwhile, the goblin flung the door of the commentary box open and began to stomp out, dragging the net of footballs behind him.

"The goblin's coming out!" Rachel exclaimed, pointing to the top of the stairs.

The girls started up the steps. They saw the goblin appear above them with the net of footballs.

Francesca

"STOP RIGHT THERE!"
Francesca shouted.

Startled, the goblin
jumped and let go
of the net. All
the footballs
tumbled out of it,
bouncing down
the steps towards
the girls.

"It's raining
footballs!" Rachel
gasped, trying to
dodge the balls.

"Look out for
Francesca's football,
Rachel!" Kirsty called,
also dodging from side
to side.

"That's fancy footwork, girls!" Francesca called approvingly as Kirsty and Rachel side-stepped the flying footballs. The goblin was rushing down the steps towards them now, trying to gather the footballs up in his arms. Then Rachel noticed that one of the footballs heading straight towards her was surrounded by tiny golden sparkles.

Francesca's Magic Football! Rachel
thought, her heart pounding with
excitement. She reached out for the
special ball, but the goblin had noticed
it at exactly the same moment. He
dropped the other balls immediately
and raced after Francesca's football.

"Get out of my way!" the goblin
yelled, shoving Rachel aside. She
stumbled, and the Magic Football

bounced past her. The goblin grabbed wildly at it, but missed.

The football bounced to the bottom of the steps, and Rachel and the goblin both raced after it. But, at that very moment, one of the stadium officials came around the corner. He spotted the Magic Football and instantly scooped it up into his arms.

So Near and Yet So Far

"Oh, no!" Rachel breathed, dismayed. She glanced at her fairy friend.

Luckily, Francesca had managed to whizz out of sight as soon as the official appeared, and she was now peeping anxiously out from behind a lock of Kirsty's hair.

"What's going on here?" the official said sternly, staring at the goblin. "We've been looking for these footballs everywhere. A ballboy is supposed to look after the balls, not lose them!"

The official thinks the goblin is a ballboy! Rachel realised. *The outfit he's wearing must be one of the official ballboy tracksuits.*

"Pick all these footballs up, please," the official went on.

Scowling, the goblin did as he was told, shoving the footballs back into the net one by one. Rachel and Kirsty began to help. *Maybe we'll still have a chance to get the Magic Football back,* Kirsty thought hopefully.

"Oh, don't bother with that, girls," the official said with a smile. "The match will be starting soon, and you don't want to miss it. Off you go."

Reluctantly, Rachel and Kirsty moved away. They watched as the official put the Magic Football into the net with the others. Then he took the net from the goblin and strode off down a corridor which led into the back of the stadium.

"Come on," he said to the goblin,
"We need to find the other ballboys
and girls."

The goblin smirked widely at Kirsty
and Rachel before skipping off after
the official.

"Oh dear," Francesca flew out from
behind Kirsty's hair, looking very glum.
"Where's he taking my football? We
have to get it back!"

"That's going to be difficult," Kirsty
said with a frown. She pointed at a
sign on the wall of the corridor which
read: PRIVATE – NO ACCESS TO THE PUBLIC.
"We won't be allowed into the official
areas of the stadium. The goblin's only
allowed in because that man thinks he's
a ballboy."

Francesca winked at her. "Well, with

a little bit of magic, anything's possible. Maybe they could use two more ballgirls..." She waved her wand and then, in a shower of dazzling fairy dust, Kirsty and Rachel's outfits changed.

Now they were both wearing dark blue tracksuits, exactly like the goblin's.

"Let's go!" Rachel cried.

The three friends hurried down the passageway. They couldn't see the goblin or the official, so they began checking the rooms along the corridor. They peeped inside them, but there was no sign of the goblin or the footballs.

Then, as they got towards the corner
of the corridor, they heard voices coming
from a room with its door ajar.

Rachel and Kirsty peeped around the
door. Inside was a large group of ballboys
and ballgirls. Each of them was holding a
football, and they were listening intently
to a man at the front of the room.

"...And remember, it's important to get

the ball back into play as soon
as possible," the man was saying.

Kirsty nudged Rachel. "There's
the net that held the footballs," she
whispered, pointing at the net which
was now lying on the floor, empty.

"But where's Francesca's Magic
Football?" Rachel whispered back,
scanning all the balls in the room for

the tell-tale sparkle of fairy magic.
"Nobody in here seems to have it."

"The goblin's not here either,"
Francesca said with a frown. "He must
have got away with my football."

"We'd better go," Kirsty murmured,
"otherwise that official might see us
and call us into the meeting."

The girls slipped quietly away down
the corridor.

"But where shall we start looking
for the goblin now?" asked Rachel.

The girls stared at each other in
desperation. But, all of a sudden,
they heard a croaky voice singing
a football chant:

"Go, goblins, go!
Boot it high,
Boot it low.

Win, goblins, win!
Stamp their toes,
Kick their shins."

"It's the goblin!" Francesca cried.

Football Fever

"After him!" Kirsty shouted.

Francesca and the girls darted around the corner of the corridor. Ahead of them they saw the goblin, still singing croakily to himself. He was running along and expertly dribbling a football ahead of him, occasionally flicking the ball up with his toe and heading it forwards.

"Wow!" Rachel panted as they chased after him. "He's better than some of the Tippington Rovers players!"

"That's the magic of my football at work," Francesca told her.

"Even dribbling that football, he's getting away from us," Kirsty pointed out as the goblin headed towards a door at the bottom of the corridor.

"Girls, you'll be much quicker if you're fairy-sized." Francesca said, raising her wand.

Rachel and Kirsty skidded to a halt, and Francesca showered them with fairy dust. They instantly shrank to become tiny fairies, with glittering wings on their backs.

As Francesca and the girls flew swiftly down the corridor together, the goblin flung the door open and skipped outside, not even bothering to close the door behind him again.

A moment later, Francesca, Kirsty and Rachel reached the door and peeked outside. "Oh, it's the stadium car park!" Rachel exclaimed.

"But where's the goblin?" asked Kirsty, staring at all the coaches and cars parked in neat rows. Lots more football fans were arriving now, too, as it was getting close to the start of the match.

"He must be somewhere in the car park," Francesca decided. "We'll have to search for him, but we mustn't let anyone see us."

Rachel and Kirsty nodded and followed Francesca high up into the air. They hovered above the car park so that they could get a good view of everything below them, but they could see no sign of the goblin anywhere.

"Maybe we should split up and search each part of the car park more carefully," Kirsty suggested.

Rachel was about to reply when her
attention was caught by a rather
strange sight. A coach was heading
very slowly towards one of the car park
exits, zig-zagging from side to side.

"Look at that coach," Rachel said
to her friends. "Why is it leaving before
the match has even started?"

"That *is* odd," Francesca agreed.

"Let's check it out," Kirsty suggested,
zooming downwards.

Rachel and Francesca followed. As the three of them drew level with the coach, they peeped in through the windows.

"It's full of goblins!" Kirsty cried, looking up and down the packed coach.

"What are they doing here?" asked Rachel anxiously.

"It's the Goblin Olympic Football Team," Francesca explained, looking worried. "They must be hoping to practise with my Magic Football."

The goblins were dressed in a white football strip which had a picture of Jack Frost on the front. They all looked extremely pleased with themselves, bouncing up and down in their seats and singing loudly:

"Go, goblins, go!
Boot it high,
Boot it low.

Win, goblins, win!
Stamp their toes,
Kick their shins."

⚙ 56 ⚙

"They're not very sporting, are they?" Francesca said, frowning. "'Kick their shins', indeed!"

"But where's the goblin with the Magic Football?" asked Kirsty.

Rachel soon spotted him. The goblin they'd been chasing was now driving the coach, his face screwed up in concentration.

"Look, girls," Francesca whispered, pointing her wand at the goblins' feet. Rachel and Kirsty glanced down and saw the Magic Football rolling around on the floor of the coach.

"Let's go and find somewhere else to practise our football skills," shouted the goblin driver to the rest of the team.

"We've wasted loads of time, though," moaned a goblin at the back of the coach. "Just because you got the Magic Football muddled up with a lot of the humans' footballs."

"Well, I found it again, didn't I?" the goblin at the wheel retorted. "Anyway, I was just checking out the stadium to find somewhere for us to practise. I didn't know some silly humans were going to be playing a match here today!"

"Can't you go any faster?" demanded another goblin.

"Yes, at this rate we won't have left the car park before the Fairyland Olympics start in six days!" another added.

"Shut up!" the goblin at the wheel snapped crossly. "We've got the Magic Football, and that's all that matters. Those pesky fairies won't stand a chance of beating us at the Fairyland Olympics!"

The goblins cheered loudly. Meanwhile, Francesca, Rachel and Kirsty looked at each other in concern.

"How are we going to get the Magic Football back?" Kirsty whispered as they hovered beside the slow-moving coach. "There are just too many goblins around!"

Rachel thought for a moment. "Maybe we can distract the driver while Francesca sneaks onto the coach and gets her football back," she suggested.

"Good idea," Francesca agreed. "When I try to pick the ball up, it will immediately shrink to its Fairyland size, but it's going to be difficult for me to get close to it while it's rolling around on the floor. You'll have to try to buy me as much time as you can, girls."

"We will!" Kirsty said in a determined voice.

Francesca pointed her wand at the driver's window and, with a few sparkles of fairy magic, it slid open a crack.

"Good luck, girls," Francesca whispered as the three of them zipped in quickly through the open window.

Kirsty and Rachel both felt very nervous as they watched Francesca zoom down towards the football. Would their plan work?

Goblins, Go Home!

"Let's give this goblin a surprise, Kirsty," Rachel whispered.

Kirsty nodded, and followed Rachel down to land on the top of the steering-wheel.

"Hello!" Rachel called, waving up at the goblin.

"Remember us?" Kirsty added.

The goblin's eyes almost popped out of his head. "Are you girls or fairies?" he asked, scratching his head in confusion. Then he let out a squeal of rage. "Ooh, you're both!" And he took his hands off the steering-wheel and began swiping furiously at the girls.

As Rachel and Kirsty dodged out of his way, the coach began to swerve wildly. Kirsty glanced down and saw that the Magic Football was rolling about all over the place. Francesca just couldn't get close to it at all.

"Look out!" Rachel gasped suddenly, as she saw the coach heading straight towards a row of parked cars.

"Hit the brakes!" Kirsty shouted.

Looking scared, the goblin slammed on the brakes. The coach shuddered to a halt, just nudging one of the cars ever so gently on its bumper. Rachel, Kirsty and the goblins breathed sighs of relief.

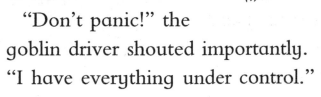

"Don't panic!" the goblin driver shouted importantly. "I have everything under control."

But, at that very moment, the airbag
inside the steering-wheel
inflated. It ballooned
out and completely
muffled the
goblin's head.

"Help!"
spluttered the
goblin. "I've
been attacked by
a giant balloon!"

But, instead of rushing to help their
friend, the other goblins on the coach
roared with laughter. Rachel and Kirsty
grinned at each other, then glanced
down at Francesca. Now that
the coach had stopped, she was able
to reach her Magic Football, and
shrank it quickly to its Fairyland size.

Beaming all over her face, Francesca scooped up her precious football and then zoomed upwards to join Rachel and Kirsty. "Thanks, girls," Francesca laughed. "Now, let's get out of here."

The three of them whizzed out of the open window again, just as the driver-goblin managed to struggle free of the airbag. He glanced down and scowled when he saw that the football had gone.

"Those fairies have stolen the Magic Football!" he shouted.

Immediately, the goblins scrambled off the coach as quickly as they could to race after Francesca and the girls. The three fairies hovered in mid-air, just out of reach.

"You goblins had better go home and start practising your football skills," Francesca said sternly, "because you won't have the Magic Football to help you now!"

The goblins moaned and grumbled when they saw the sparkling football tucked safely under Francesca's arm.

"Why didn't you stop them taking the football?" shouted the driver-goblin to his friends.

"Don't blame us!" the other goblins muttered. "This is all your fault!"

"Off you go, back to Fairyland," said Francesca.

The goblins muttered grumpily and stuck out their tongues at Francesca and the girls, but they stomped off.

"They've got a lot of football practice to do now," Francesca said with a grin.

"But if they do win at the fairy games,
at least they'll have won fair and
square. And now I must go straight
back to Fairyland and tell everyone
the good news, but first, there are
a few things I must put right…"

Francesca touched the Magic Football
with her wand, and a sparkling burst of

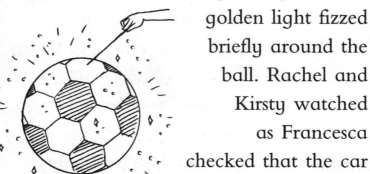

golden light fizzed
briefly around the
ball. Rachel and
Kirsty watched
as Francesca
checked that the car
the coach had bumped
into wasn't damaged. Then she pointed
her wand at the coach and a burst of
fairy dust surrounded it, rolling it gently
back into an empty parking space.

Finally, Francesca led Rachel and Kirsty
back into the football stadium, where
another cloud of fairy dust turned
the girls back to their normal sizes and
returned them to their original outfits.

"Thank you again, girls," Francesca
said, her eyes twinkling. "Everything
will be fine with the Tippington and
Alton match now, and it's just about
to start, so go and enjoy yourselves!"

Rachel and Kirsty waved as Francesca shot upwards. "Goodbye," they called.

Francesca waved back and blew the girls a kiss. Then, with a cheeky smile, she began dribbling her Magic Football from toe to toe in mid-air. Next second, she and the football both vanished in a cloud of fairy sparkles.

"We can really enjoy the match, Kirsty," Rachel said happily as they rushed back to their seats, "now that we know Francesca has her football back."

Kirsty grinned and nodded. "Yes, and let's hope Tippington Rovers win," she cheered.

The Sporty Fairies

Rachel and Kirsty must now help

Zoe the Skating Fairy

Jack Frost's scheming goblins have stolen
Zoe's Magic Lace and are using it to
improve their chances of winning the
Fairyland Olympics! Can Rachel and
Kirsty help Zoe to get it back?

Skating Struggles

Rachel Walker held on tightly to the
park railings as she stood up on her
in-line skates. "Whoa-a-a!" she laughed,
as her feet moved slightly in different
directions. "How are you getting
on, Kirsty?"

Kirsty Tate, Rachel's best friend, was
still sitting on the grass, tying the laces
on her skates. She fastened the top
straps, then smiled up at Rachel. Kirsty
was staying with Rachel's family for a
week during the Easter holidays, and
today the girls had come to Oval Park,
near the Walkers' house.

"All right...I think," Kirsty replied, clutching Rachel's hand and standing up. Then she grinned. "We must be mad to be skating today after everything that's happened to the Sporty Fairies," she said, wobbling on her wheels.

"At least we're well-protected," Rachel reminded her, tapping on Kirsty's helmet. "And this is such a good place to skate, I'm sure we'll still have fun."

The girls certainly were well-protected – with helmets, knee pads and elbow pads, just in case either of them took a tumble. And Rachel was right, the park was perfect for skating, with its wide path looping around the edge, where lots of skaters and skateboarders were trying out their skills. It was a warm sunny day, with a fresh breeze just rustling through the leaves in the trees, and making the daffodils nod their yellow heads.

Unfortunately, there seemed to be a lot of bumps and falls taking place amongst the skaters today. This was because Zoe the Skating Fairy's Magic Lace was missing. That meant skaters and skateboarders everywhere were having trouble...

Read the rest of

Zoe the Skating Fairy

to find out what magic happens next...

Have you ever wanted to name
your own Rainbow Magic Fairy?

Now is your chance to help us choose
the most magical, sparkly name
for a Rainbow Magic Fairy!*

Log on to www.rainbowmagic.co.uk
to unlock the magic within!

www.rainbowmagic.co.uk is the place to
go for games, downloads, competitions,
activities, latest news, and lots of fun!

Plus meet the fairies and find out
about their amazing adventures
with Rachel and Kirsty.

* Competition runs from April 2008 for four weeks –
please see www.rainbowmagic.co.uk for more details
For terms and conditions please see www.hachettechildrens.co.uk/terms

Win Rainbow Magic goodies!

In every book in the Rainbow Magic Sporty Fairies series
(books 57-63) there is a hidden picture of a hoop with a secret letter
in it. Find all seven letters and re-arrange them to make
a special Sporty Fairies word, then send it to us. Each month we
will put the entries into a draw and select one winner to receive
a Rainbow Magic Sparkly T-shirt and Goody Bag!

Send your entry on a postcard to Rainbow Magic Sporty Fairies
Competition, Orchard Books, 338 Euston Road, London NW1 3BH.
Australian readers should write to Hachette Children's Books,
Level 17/207 Kent Street, Sydney, NSW 2000.
New Zealand readers should write to Rainbow Magic Competition,
4 Whetu Place, Mairangi Bay, Auckland, NZ. Don't forget to
include your name and address. Only one entry per child.
Final draw: 30th April 2009.

Good luck!

Look out for the Music Fairies!

POPPY
THE PIANO FAIRY
978-1-40830-033-6

ELLIE
THE GUITAR FAIRY
978-1-40830-030-5

FIONA
THE FLUTE FAIRY
978-1-40830-029-9

DANNI
THE DRUM FAIRY
978-1-40830-028-2

MAYA
THE HARP FAIRY
978-1-40830-031-2

VICTORIA
THE VIOLIN FAIRY
978-1-40830-027-5

SADIE
THE SAXOPHONE FAIRY
978-1-40830-032-9

Available
September 2008